The Children of Green Knowe

ALSO BY L. M. BOSTON

Treasure of Green Knowe
The River at Green Knowe
A Stranger at Green Knowe
An Enemy at Green Knowe

The Castle of Yew
The Sea Egg
Nothing Said